T5-CVH-985

The Story of
CHRISTMAS
A Coloring Book for Children

Text
Roberta Letwenko

Cover Illustration
Michael Letwenko

Text Illustrations
Edward Letwenko

REGINA PRESS
New York

Copyright © 1988 by The Regina Press
All rights reserved. No part of this book may be reproduced in any form
without permission in writing from the publisher.

Long ago, a young woman named Mary lived in a small town called Nazareth. She was good and holy and filled with the love of God.

One day, while she was praying, an angel came to her.
He said, "Hail, Mary. You are full of grace. God has
chosen you to be the mother of His son. You are to
name the baby Jesus."
Mary said to the angel, "I shall do what God wants."
And the angel left her.

Not long after, Mary married a man named Joseph. He was a good and holy man.

Joseph was a carpenter, and Mary would come to visit
him. Every day he worked hard in his shop where he
made things out of wood.

The people of Nazareth came to buy the things that Joseph made in his shop.

One day a soldier came to Nazareth from far-off Rome and told the men and women that the King in Rome wanted to count his people. He said they should go to their home towns where they would be counted.

Joseph belonged to a family that was started by David.
Bethlehem was David's family town.

Mary and Joseph set out for their home town
Bethlehem. The journey was long and hard.

Bethlehem was a noisy, crowded place. People and animals filled the busy streets.

Mary was very tired and Joseph tried to find a place for her to rest. He went to the town's one small inn. "I'm sorry," said the inn's owner, "All the homes and inns are filled. I have no room left. But you might find a place to sleep outside the town."

Joseph and Mary went to the country places at the edge of the town. There they found a cave that was used as a stable and where animals were kept. The cave was warm and dry.

In that cave Mary and Joseph were able to rest at last
while Mary waited for the baby the angel had promised.

In the night, Mary's baby was born. She wrapped Him in cloths to keep him warm and laid Him in the soft hay in the manger. She adored the tiny child and remembered that the angel had said, "He shall be the Son of God."

That night God sent his angel to some poor men who were watching their sheep in a field close by. The angel said, "Do not be afraid! I bring you wonderful news. Tonight in Bethlehem a baby has been born. This child is Christ the Lord. You will find Him wrapped in cloths and lying in a manger."

Then more angels came and filled the sky with light. They sang, "Glory to God in the highest, and peace on earth among men." Then they went away.

The shepherds looked in wonder. One of them said,
"Let us go to Bethlehem and find the child the angels
told us about."

The shepherds found the Christ child in the cave and were happy to see Him. They wanted to tell everyone the good news.

In the town they stopped people and told them what they had seen. They told about the angels and about the baby who was Christ the Lord. They told about Mary, his mother. The people were happy about the good news.

When the baby was eight days old, Mary and Joseph
named Him Jesus as the angel had told Mary to do. They
took Jesus to the temple in Jerusalem to make an
offering to God.

They were very poor, so all they could buy was two
small birds for their offering.

A man named Simeon saw Jesus in the temple. He had been waiting a long time for God to send His Son. He held the child and said, "Lord, this child will be a light to the world and the glory of your people."

A woman named Anna also was praying in the temple that day. She was asking God to send Christ to the world.

When Anna saw Jesus, she knew He was God's Son. She was very happy and ran to tell the good news to everyone she met.

Far to the East, some men were studying the stars. A bright new star appeared on the night Jesus was born. They looked in some old books to find out what the star meant. The books said, "A new star will shine in the sky when a great King is born to the Jewish people."

One of the Wise men said, "Let us go to see this king.
The star will show us the way." Riding their camels,
they followed the bright star to Jerusalem. With them
they carried gifts for the baby.

In Jerusalem the Wise men saw Herod, the ruler of the
Jews. They asked him where they could find the child
who was born King of the Jews. Herod's priests told
them, "It is said He will be born in Bethlehem." Herod
told the Wise men, "Find the child and let me know
where He is, so I can adore Him."

But the wicked Herod was very angry. He wanted to be the only King of the Jews. He thought, "If I find this child, I shall have Him killed."

The Wise men followed the star to the cave in Bethlehem. They went inside and saw Mary, Joseph, and the baby Jesus. They worshipped the tiny child and gave him rich gifts. That night an angel warned them not to return to Herod for he wanted to harm the child.

Also that night an angel came to Joseph in a dream. The angel told him to take Mary and the child to Egypt where they would be safe from the wicked Herod.

Joseph told Mary what the angel had said. At once, they started out for Egypt, where they stayed until Herod died.

After Herod died, Joseph and Mary took Jesus back to live in Nazareth, their home town. There Jesus went to school, learned to be a carpenter and grew into manhood.